The First Dog

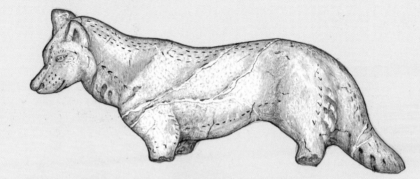

The First Dog

Written and illustrated by Jan Brett

Voyager Books • Harcourt, Inc.

Orlando Austin New York San Diego Toronto London

Publisher's note

Between 35,000 and 12,000 years ago, as the last of the great glaciers of the Pleistocene advanced and retreated over the grasslands of Europe and the New World, people like ourselves — *Homo sapiens sapiens*— began to flourish. Hunters and gatherers, they wore clothes made of animal skins, had shell and bone ornaments, and used such tools as spears and knives. They made music and were prolific artists. This was a time of exceptional artistic achievement and technological advance, and it may have been during this period that the first wild animals were domesticated.

Jan Brett has created an appealing story from this possibility, setting it in a breathtaking Ice Age landscape populated with animals that coexisted with early man in Europe and the New World. The images and ornaments of her borders were inspired by the cave paintings and artifacts surviving from this time.

For Ronny and Tom Waters
and Daniel Droller

Requests for permission to make copies of any part of the work should be mailed to the following address: Permissions Department, Harcourt, Inc., 6277 Sea Harbor Drive, Orlando, Florida 32887-6777.

Voyager Books is a registered trademark of Harcourt, Inc.

The Library of Congress has cataloged the hardcover edition as follows:
Brett, Jan, 1949–
The first dog/by Jan Brett.
p. cm.
Summary: Kip the cave boy and Paleowolf each face hunger and danger on a journey in Paleolithic times: when they decide to join forces and help one another, Paleowolf becomes the first dog.
[1. Dogs — Fiction. 2. Prehistoric animals — Fiction. 3. Man, Prehistoric— Fiction.] I. Title.
PZ7.B7559F1 1988 [E]—dc19 88-2224
ISBN 0-15-227650-5
ISBN 0-15-227651-3 pb
ISBN 0-15-201967-7 oversize pb
Printed by South China Printing Co., Ltd., China
T S R Q P O N M

Manufactured in China

LONG, LONG AGO in the great days of the Pleistocene, Kip
the cave boy bounded down the trail on his way home.

He avoided the Aurochs, the Cave Bears, and the Megaceros. He evaded the Woolly Rhinoceros, the Wild Horse, and the Mighty Mammoth.

But he was getting tired and hungry and he was still a long way from home.

He marched on until he saw a great rock. It was a good place to stop and rest. Kip reached in his bag for a Woolly Rhino rib, still sweet and smoky from his fire.

Suddenly, up popped a Paleowolf, looking for leftovers. Wolf's nose began to twitch and sniff. He sniffed to the left and he sniffed to the right.

"What are you doing?" teased Kip. "What can you smell in this emptiness?"

Paleowolf held his snout high in the air. With his keen nose, he could smell:

a rain cloud across the valley,

the track of a tiny toad,

the pelt of a prying pachyderm.

But most of all, he could smell roasted Woolly Rhino bones, and he gave a hungry whine.

"Pooh," said Kip. "I can't smell anything but my dinner, and it is all for me." And he turned his back on Wolf.

But Paleowolf had already hurried away. And when Kip saw the reason why, he was just able to get away in time.

Soon Kip was back on the homeward trail. He walked on and on until he spied a cave. It was a fine place to stop and rest. He thought about another Rhino rib, still crackly and crunchy from the fire.

Up popped Paleowolf, looking for leftovers.

Wolf's ears began to turn and dip. He listened to the left and he listened to the right.

"What are you doing?" mocked Kip, taking a big bite. "What can you hear in this silence?"

Wolf cocked his head. With his fine canine ears, he could hear:

a fish rise in the river,

a leaf fall,

the soft pant, pant, pant of a Cave Bear.

But most of all, he could hear the snap of Woolly Rhino bones, still crisp from the fire. And he gave a pleading howl.

"Pooh," said Kip. "I can't hear anything, except my teeth crunching on these very tasty bones." And he threw a clump of moss at Paleowolf.

But Paleowolf had already hurried away. And when Kip saw the reason why, he was just able to get away in time.

Soon Kip was back on the homeward trail, more footsore and weary than ever. He trudged on and on until he saw a big tree. It was just the place to stop and rest. He climbed the tree and reached for a Woolly Rhino rib, still pearly and greasy from the fire.

Up popped Paleowolf, looking for leftovers.

Wolf's eyes began to sparkle and dance. He looked to the left and he looked to the right.

"What are you doing?" jeered Kip. "What can you see in this darkness?"

Wolf's eyes glowed. With his sharp eyes he could see:
    the shimmer of a distant drop of dew,
    a mouse scurrying, far away,
    a feline sleeping high above.
    But most of all he could see a pearly, greasy morsel of
Rhino bone, shining in the moonlight, and he licked his
chops.

"Pooh," said Kip. "I can't see anything, except of course my roasted, toasted, crispy crunchy, pearly, greasy Woolly Rhino rib. And you won't be tasting that, because I want it all to myself."

Then Kip yelled, "SHOOOO!" as loud as he could.

The yell resounded up and down the tree. It woke every living thing around.

Instantly Paleowolf's nose wrinkled and his ears went back. His eyes narrowed and his tail stood out. He looked so terrible that Kip threw the whole bag of Rhino ribs down from the tree. "Help yourself, Wolfy!"

But Paleowolf did not care about dinner now. His mane bristled and ridged down his back. A long growl shook from his throat. It was his last warning.

Kip opened his eyes very wide. He looked all around,
but he could not smell, or hear, or see anything.

He whispered, "What do you know, wise Wolf?"

But Paleowolf was gone.

There is great danger here, thought Kip. I must
disappear, too. And he shrank into the leafy branches and
made himself very small.

Just in time. For high in the tree was the most fearsome of creatures — the Saber-Toothed Cat. She crouched, she snarled, and then she sprang.

She hurtled past Kip, hidden in the leaves, and
pounced on the pile of Woolly Rhino bones down below.

All that night, as he sat in the tree, Kip thought and thought. He shivered over Paleowolf's last warning. It had not been one second too soon.

The next morning, Kip climbed down. There was Paleowolf, looking for leftovers. Together they looked at the spot where the bones had been, and they were very gloomy.

Finally, Kip made a speech. He said: "Wolfy, if you will use your keen nose and your fine ears and your sharp eyes to keep me from being eaten up, I promise to share with you all the Woolly Rhino ribs and even Mammoth meat that I cook over my fire."

Paleowolf barked, meaning "Yes." And then he wagged his tail, the very first wolf to do so.

When Kip saw that, he cried, "And I will call you 'Dog,' which means 'One who wags his tail.'"

Then Kip the cave boy and the first dog went on home.